HOW DO YOU FEEL?

FOR KOTARO

The author would like to thank the Illustration Institute for providing creative time and space at the Marilyn Faison Artist Residency on Peaks Island, Maine, during the summers of 2017 and 2018.

And special thanks to the children and staff of the Adam J. Lewis Academy in Bridgeport, Connecticut, for their expert advice and inspiration.

Printed and bound in May 2019 at Toppan Leefung, DongGuan City, China.

The artwork was created with acrylics on gessoed aluminum composite board.

www.holidayhouse.com

First Edition

1 3 5 7 9 10 8 6 4 2

Library of Congress Cataloging-in-Publication Data

Names: Rockwell, Lizzy, author.

Title: How do you feel? / Lizzy Rockwell.

Description: First edition. | New York : Holiday House, [2019]

Identifiers: LCCN 2019000879 | ISBN 9780823440511 (hardcover)

Subjects: LCSH: Emotions in children—Juvenile literature. | Emotions—Juvenile literature.

Classification: LCC BF723.E6 R634 2019 | DDC 155.4/124—dc23

LC record available at https://lccn.loc.gov/2019000879

HOW DO YOU FEEL?

LIZZY ROCKWELL

HOLIDAY HOUSE · NEW YORK

How do you feel?

Do you feel happy?

Do you feel sad?

Do you feel silly?

Do you feel mad?

Do you feel sorry?

Do you feel scared?

Do you feel calm?

Do you feel brave?

Do you feel shy?

Do you feel friendly?

How do you feel?

Happy

Sad

Sorry

Scared

Shy